CONTENTS

MEET BUG TEAM ALPHA

Bug Team Alpha is the most elite Special Operations force of the Colonial Armed Forces of the Earth Colonial Coalition. Each member has an insect's DNA surgically grafted onto his or her human DNA. With special abilities and buglike features, these soldiers are trained to tackle the most dangerous and unique combat missions. Their home base is *Space Station Prime*.

Jackson "Vision" Boone

A human male with large eye grafts that resemble fly eyes. The eyes allow detection of multiple light spectra beyond human perception.

Rank. Commander
Age. 29 Earth Standard Years
Place of Origin. Planet Hephaestus
Hair. Light brown
Eyes. Fly eye graft
Height. 1.83 metres (6 feet)

Irene "Impact" Mallory

A human female with a beetle exoskeleton grafted onto her body. She's always slightly hunched over, like a linebacker ready to charge an opponent.

Rank. Lieutenant
Age. 24 Earth Standard Years
Place of Origin. Earth, European Hemisphere
Hair. Brown
Eyes. Brown
Height. 1.68 metres (5 feet, 6 inches)

Akiko "Radar" Murasaki

A human female with cranial antennae grafted onto her forehead. The antennae sense vibrations and can determine length between and shape of objects in dark spaces.

Rank. Lieutenant
Age. 28 Earth Standard Years
Place of Origin. Earth, Asian Hemisphere
Hair. Brown
Eyes. Brown
Height. 1.58 metres (5 feet, 2 inches)

Sancho "Locust" Castillo

A human male with wings and a dorsal exoskeleton grafted onto his body. He has immense strength and flying capabilities.

Rank. Lieutenant
Age. 23 Earth Standard Years
Place of Origin. Earth,
    South American Hemisphere
Hair. Light brown
Eyes. Brown
Height. 1.83 metres [6 feet]

Madhuri "Scorpion" Singh

A human female with spikes grafted onto her body. She can knock out an enemy with her venom.

Rank. Lieutenant
Age. 24 Earth Standard Years
Place of Origin. Earth Colony Shiva
    Three
Hair. Brown
Eyes. Brown
Height. 1.80 metres [5 feet,
    11 inches]

Gustav "Burrow" Von Braun

A human male with digger beetle arms grafted onto his torso. He is heavyset and very muscular.

Rank. Lieutenant
Age. 24 Earth Standard Years
Place of Origin. Earth,
    European Hemisphere
Hair. Brown
Eyes. Brown
Height. 1.68 metres [5 feet,
    6 inches]

Liu "Hopper" Yu

A human male with grasshopper legs grafted onto his hips. Footpads take the place of footwear. He is slender and always springy, ready to jump.

Rank. Lieutenant
Age. 21 Earth Standard Years
Place of Origin. Earth,
    Asian Hemisphere
Hair. None, head is shaved
Eyes. Brown
Height. 1.88 metres [6 feet, 2 inches]

CHAPTER 1

Lessa McCaffrey, the President of Earth, sat with her advisers aboard the presidential spacecraft, *Space Ship One*. They were en route to the planet Delphus for a special summit meeting. Representatives from all planetary colonies and allies of the Earth Colonial Coalition were gathering to discuss the increasing aggression of the Draco, a reptilian species from the planet Dracos with a taste for war.

President McCaffrey ran a hand through her short, silvery grey hair. Her face was etched with worry lines carved by 10 Earth Standard years in office. She was a short, plump woman, but her small body contained a robust energy. During her term in office, she had faced many challenges, but the Draco were proving to be the most troublesome.

"Within the last eight Earth Standard months, the Draco have taken over four star systems claimed by the Earth Colonial Coalition," President McCaffrey summarized.

The president sat back in her chair at the private conference table. She straightened the folds in her uniform as she spoke, as if that would straighten out the problems with the Draco.

"Clearly they aren't satisfied with completely conquering their own region of space. Now they want to branch out into Coalition territory," Dyanna LeGuin, one of the president's advisers, observed.

LeGuin was a tall, slender woman with waves of long blonde hair. She fidgeted in her chair as she discussed the Draco. She did not like to sit still for long periods of time. She stood up and paced around the conference table with her hands clasped behind her back.

"It's what they do. The Draco have been a warrior culture for thousands of years," Ramona Fraydon, a second adviser, mentioned.

Fraydon was relaxed in contrast to energetic LeGuin. They were a good balance for McCaffrey.

"We've been watching the Draco since we first encountered the species, but they hadn't bothered our territories," Fraydon continued. "We didn't consider them much of a threat."

"Well, they're bothering us now," LeGuin said. "And they don't show any signs of stopping."

"Fortunately, none of the planets they've invaded in our territory were occupied. No colonists are currently endangered," the president said. "That's why I haven't dispatched the Colonial Armed Forces. Yet."

"But there are inhabited planetary colonies now within striking distance of the Draco's forces. The Armed Forces might have to get involved," Fraydon observed.

"That's what this summit is about. We have to join together and discuss how to approach this threat," the president said. "Do we send diplomats or troops?"

Suddenly, the ship shuddered and lurched. The president was almost thrown out of her chair. Alarms went off. Two Protective Service agents, a tall man and a petite woman – code names Vesuvius and Pompeii – immediately entered the meeting room. They locked the door and flanked the president.

"What happened?" McCaffrey asked.

"There has been an explosion in the engine room. We've dropped out of hyperspace," Agent Pompeii reported. "We believe we are being sabotaged."

A new sound vibrated through the ship's bulkheads. McCaffrey recognized it.

"We're being fired upon!" the president shouted.

Both of the Protective Service agents listened to something on their security comms. Then they started to rush the president from the room.

"We've got to get you to Escape Pod One, ma'am. We've been ambushed by Draco ships," Agent Vesuvius revealed. "They're attempting to board."

Space Ship One had many escape pods, but only one was equipped with a special emergency comm and locator beacon. It also had a small hyperdrive engine. Once inside the pod, McCaffrey could navigate away from an attack and call for aid.

She did not make it to the pod.

Blaster fire erupted as soon as the president stepped out of the meeting room. The Protective Service agents shoved the president to the deck and leaped in front of her like human shields. They returned fire, but were hit by the enemy. As they fell, President McCaffrey got her first, real-life look at the Draco.

The Draco warriors were humanoid with two arms, two legs, a torso and a head, but they had reptilian faces and skin. Their eyes were narrow and very brightly coloured. They had snouts instead of noses. She couldn't see if they had ears under their combat helmets.

Their bodies were covered in battle gear that looked vaguely like ancient samurai armour. It consisted of a solid chest plate moulded to the shape of the soldier's torso, along with arm guards and shin guards made from strips of metal laced together. Metal boots stomped close to her face.

Even though the Draco were armed with energy blasters, McCaffrey saw that the soldiers wore slim, curved swords attached to their belts.

McCaffrey had seen holo-pics of the Draco during briefings and intel reports, but that was nothing compared to coming face to face with them, or looking into the barrel of one of their weapons.

"Up," one of the Draco soldiers said.

The president got to her feet. She did not raise her hands in surrender.

"Move," the soldier instructed and gestured for her to walk.

President McCaffrey, now separated from her advisers and her unconscious Protective Service agents, reluctantly followed the Draco's orders. One soldier jabbed her in the chest with his weapon, guiding her to the hull breach where the Draco had invaded *Space Ship One*.

Along the way she passed members of the crew and staff being rounded up and held under vigilant guard by Draco soldiers. She was taken to an airlock tube that now connected *Space Ship One* to a Draco vessel.

The soldiers escorted President McCaffrey across the airlock and onto the Draco ship. There, she was met by the Draco commander and even more soldiers.

The Draco commander was dressed in elaborate ceremonial armour. It had many layers of polished metal plates and swaths of colourful fabric dripping with battle awards and medals. He also wore a helmet that flared out at the sides like dragon wings. Twin swords attached to his belt formed an X at his waist.

McCaffrey thought the Draco commander's attire was a bit much, but she reminded herself that this was a warrior culture. Rank was important to them. The commander was definitely displaying his importance to her.

"Greetings, valued captive," the Draco said. "I am Histaah, the Supreme Commander of the Dracos Space Fleet. The President of Earth is a worthy prize. You will bring me much honour and victory."

McCaffrey did not speak back to him. Her only response was an intense glare, showing only toughness, not fear.

"Get the rest of the Earth Colonial Coalition survivors and bring them aboard my flagship," Histaah ordered several other soldiers standing nearby. "I want all of them to witness my supreme authority."

The Draco soldiers quickly dispersed. Moments later they marched back onto the flagship with the remaining passengers and crew from *Space Ship One* along with the other soldiers who had been standing guard over them. The new hostages were now gathered around President McCaffrey.

The president did a quick head count of her crew. There were 23 survivors, including herself, out of the 25 people she knew had been on board *Space Ship One*.

She could only guess what had happened to the two who were missing.

"This will be your fate if you do not obey," Histaah declared as he activated a monitor screen for them to observe *Space Ship One* dead in space – just before it blew up.

The abrupt loss of all signals from *Space Ship One* set off alarms at both the Coalition presidential headquarters back on Earth and on *Space Station Prime*, the headquarters of the Colonial Armed Forces in orbit above the planet. Vice President Standing Eagle called General Barrett, the commander of the Colonial Armed Forces, and asked for an explanation.

"What happened to *Space Ship One*?" the vice president asked via a secure video comm link.

"We're investigating, sir," Barrett replied from his office on *Space Station Prime*. "I've sent Coalition ships to the last known coordinates."

An aide suddenly burst into the vice president's office. She was from a Coalition water world named

Pacificos. She was usually a very calm person, but now she was flustered. Her normally blue skin was as pale as ice.

"Eshaya! What is . . . ?" Standing Eagle frowned at the interruption.

"Mr Vice President! We're getting a transmission from President McCaffrey!" Eshaya blurted.

"Show it to me!" both the vice president and general instructed in unison.

Eshaya's blue webbed fingers fumbled with the controls of her hand-held mobile monitor. She nervously struggled to transfer the message to the two separate screens being viewed by the vice president and the general.

"The signal has been relayed multiple times. There's a lot of interference," she said.

"I am Lessa McCaffrey, the President of Earth," the audio crackled.

Then an image came into focus. The distinguished features of the president appeared.

"I am a prisoner of the Draco," President McCaffrey continued. "I am instructed to say that I will be released only if the Earth Colonial Coalition withdraws from the planets newly claimed by the Draco."

Then the image of Draco Supreme Commander Histaah filled the monitor screen.

"Your leader will be killed if our demands are not met," Histaah stated. "You have two days to comply."

The transmission ended abruptly.

"This is ransom!" the vice president exclaimed.

"Yes. And the Draco will probably kill her even if we do meet their demands," General Barrett said. "But I have a plan to rescue the President of Earth, and it begins with Bug Team Alpha."

CHAPTER 2

Space Station Prime was the headquarters for General Barrett and the Colonial Armed Forces. It was also the home base for the Special Operations team, Bug Team Alpha.

Not only were Bug Team Alpha trained for unique and unusual missions, their bodies were specially designed for it. Each member had a different insect's DNA surgically grafted onto his or her human DNA. It gave each of them special powers. It also gave each one of them specific insectlike appearances and abilities.

Immediately after receiving the threat from the Draco commander, General Barrett assembled a strike team from the roster of the Bug Team's extraordinary operatives. It included:

— — — — — — — — —

Commander Jackson "Vision" Boone: Compound Eye DNA graft. Detection of multiple light spectra beyond human perception. Age: 29 Earth Standard Years. Planet of origin: Earth Colony Hephaestus.

— — — — — — — — —

Lt Akiko "Radar" Murasaki: Cranial Antennae DNA graft. Vibration detection. Age: 28 Earth Standard Years. Planet of origin: Earth, Asian Hemisphere.

— — — — — — — — —

Lt Irene "Impact" Mallory: Beetle Exoskeleton DNA graft. High-impact tolerance and strength. Age: 25 Earth Standard Years. Planet of origin: Earth, European Hemisphere.

— — — — — — — — —

Lt Sancho "Locust" Castillo: Locust DNA graft. Wings and dorsal exoskeleton. Heavy-duty flight and strength. Age: 23 Earth Standard Years. Planet of origin: Earth, South American Hemisphere.

Lt Liu "Hopper" Yu: Grasshopper DNA graft. Leaping ability. Age: 21 Earth Standard Years. Planet of origin: Earth, Asian Hemisphere.

Lt Madhuri "Scorpion" Singh: Scorpion DNA graft. Scorpion thumb spikes; scorpion venom modified to knock out enemy, not poison. Age: 24 Earth Standard Years. Planet of origin: Earth Colony Shiva Three.

Lt Gustav "Burrow" Von Braun: Digger Beetle arm and leg flange DNA graft. Enhanced tunnelling abilities and strength. Age: 24 Earth Standard Years. Planet of origin: Earth, European Hemisphere.

✷ ✷ ✷

After fifteen Earth Standard hours, Bug Team Alpha dropped out of hyperspace on the border of Earth Colonial Coalition and Draco territory in a stealth ship. Commander Jackson "Vision" Boone navigated the small vessel into the added cover of an asteroid field to await further instructions from General Barrett.

Commander Vision sat in the cockpit. He monitored the secure command comm chatter going back and forth between General Barrett and the armada of Coalition battleships.

The general was leading the Coalition battleships towards Dracos, the home planet of the Draco. Coalition spies operating on the planet knew that the president and the survivors of *Space Ship One* had been taken to Dracos. They just did not know exactly where on Dracos. That was the information Bug Team Alpha waited to receive. Once they had it, the Bug Team's mission was to find their way to President McCaffrey by whatever means necessary and secretly rescue her under the cover of an all-out assault unleashed by General Barrett from orbit.

In the back of the stealth ship, Scorpion, Locust, Burrow and Impact distracted themselves by playing cards. Hopper fidgeted his long grasshopper legs, as usual. Scorpion tapped her venomous spikes on the table impatiently. Radar studied intel about the enemy on her wrist computer.

"Dracos looks like it's mostly swamp," Radar reported to her teammates. "Perfect for a reptilian species, I suppose. Their tech is on a par with Coalition technology. They're space faring and have energy weapons. But they also still use bladed weapons like swords and spears."

"How quaint," Impact scoffed. "I'll choose a blaster over a blade any day."

"Heads up, team. I'm getting navigational coordinates in on a secure channel from General Barrett," Vision said from the cockpit. "President McCaffrey has been located in a maximum-security prison fortress."

"A prison? Is there a plan to get inside?" Radar asked.

"Is there a plan to get out?" Locust added.

"The information is coming in now," Vision replied. "Intel received. Transferring to your wrist computers."

"Um, the details on this infiltration route are a little thin, sir," Impact noticed as she scanned the information.

"It's nothing the Bug Team can't handle," Vision replied confidently.

"It'll keep us on our toes!" Hopper said with a wink. "Let's go!"

Bug Team Alpha arrived on the planet Dracos, somewhere near the planet's prison, in the middle of the night. Their ship was equipped with sensor-scrambling stealth shields, and the cover of darkness added another layer.

Commander Vision had a difficult time finding a solid piece of ground to land on. The terrain was marshy, and most of the soil was too soft to support the ship. When the commander finally found a dry patch, it was quite far from the prison.

Before the Bug Team members deployed from the ship, they activated their own individual stealth gear. A personal stealth field, similar to what cloaked their ship, made them appear like a blur to normal sight.

Special eyewear let the Bug Team members see each other through the stealth fields, but did not interfere with their normal sight.

Commander Vision did not need special glasses. His DNA-enhanced compound bug eyes could see his teammates as clear as day in the Dracos night, with or without their stealth fields.

To assure their invisibility, the Bug Team Alpha members turned off their helmet lights. The team also switched their comm mics to stealth mode. This allowed them to whisper yet still be heard by their teammates.

"You've all been briefed on the op," Commander Vision said. "We have one Earth Standard hour to infiltrate and reach our position of attack inside the prison before the Coalition armada starts its bombardment on the place."

"That'll stir things up," Impact mentioned.

"That's the point, lieutenant. Use the confusion to our advantage," Vision revealed. "All right, team – double check weapons, backups, Emergency Medical Packs."

"Check!"

"Check!"

"Check!" the team replied.

"Bug Team Alpha, deploy," Commander Vision said as he opened the ship's hatch.

The team stepped out onto the mucky soil of the planet Dracos and immediately gagged on the thick odours of the swamp air.

"Augh! Where was the intel about this smell?" Scorpion gasped.

The team could see the massive bulk of the prison in the distance across the wide marsh. The fortress was a giant cube without windows or any lights on the outside that they could see. The structure was a giant shadow in the night.

The planet Dracos had a few moons, but none of them were bright enough to shed light on the landscape and guide the Bug Team to their goal. However, the lack of light kept the team hidden.

"Move out," Commander Vision said and led his team into the swamp.

The team sloshed through the ankle-deep water. Their passage disturbed the decomposing vegetation and released a rotten stink. Hopper's insect footpads prevented him from wearing boots. He had to walk barefoot through the muck. It was not pleasant.

Impact struggled with every step. Normally her tough beetlelike carapace was an asset in battle. Now it was a hindrance. Its weight made her sink into the marshy sludge.

Heavyset Locust had the same trouble. He could have flown above the muck, but his wings made a distinctive buzzing sound that could alert the enemy to his presence. To maintain the safety of his team, Locust kept a low profile on the ground.

Every few metres Burrow used his arms to dig through the upper layers of mud to search for stable soil. He wanted to be able to tunnel underground to the infiltration point, but was not successful. All he did was disturb the already-smelly surroundings.

Vision and Radar scanned ahead for guard outposts, Vision with his super-sensitive eyesight and Radar with her vibration-sensing cranial antennae.

The team's intel about the location of the prison's defences was spotty. All the team knew was that there were guards posted around the perimeter. There had been no mention of a fence or barrier. Commander Vision was starting to think that the swamp was a natural obstacle for any prisoners trying to escape.

"I'm getting vibrations. Multiple Draco," Radar announced quietly as her cranial antennae quivered.

Vision halted his team immediately. The prison fortress was still at least a half-kilometre away.

"I see them," Vision confirmed. "Three Draco soldiers. They're in a bunker 80 metres out. Looks like a plasticrete block construction."

"There are two more bunkers. They're spaced about 40 metres apart. Three Draco in each," Radar said.

"I can take them, sir. Swift and silent," Scorpion said confidently. She deployed her thumb spikes to show that she was ready for action.

"I don't want to engage the enemy too soon and alert them to our presence," the commander decided. "Those bunkers have to be built on top of solid soil. Burrow, can we dig under them from here?"

Burrow tested a section of the ground nearby and gave the commander a thumbs-up. Then he started to tunnel with the full force of his digger-beetle DNA-enhanced arm and leg spikes. Moments later the rest of Bug Team Alpha followed him underground.

CHAPTER 3

"Helmet lights on!" Vision ordered as the Bug Team followed Burrow through the narrow tunnel he was creating. His burrowing action threw back big globs of slushy soil. Splat! Wet muck hit the commander in the face.

"Visors down," the commander added.

"I think the smell down here is worse than it was topside," Scorpion said.

"I think you're right. Deploy oxygen masks," Vision instructed.

The Bug Team worked their way through the dense layers of peat that made up the only solid portions of the nearby landscape. As the team crawled on their bellies in the dark, their helmet lights only illuminated the things closest to each team member – the boot heels of the person in front of them.

Vision kept one DNA-enhanced eye on his wrist computer. He wanted to make sure Burrow stayed on course for the coordinates of the infiltration point. None of them knew exactly what they'd find when they got there. They only knew that it was a way into the prison fortress.

"Oh, yuck!" Hopper moaned over the comm. "There are big slimy worms down here."

"At least it isn't spiders," Radar said under her breath.

"Worms are good for the health of the soil," Burrow said. "They're part of the ecosystem."

"Ugh. The sooner I'm out of this ecosystem the better," Hopper grumbled.

Suddenly, the soil that Burrow was digging through collapsed, and water rushed into the tunnel. Mud and ooze poured over the Bug Team. Visibility turned to zero in a few seconds. Their oxygen masks were the only things that kept them from drowning as Burrow dug furiously through the muck, searching for the surface.

The team emerged from the flooded tunnel and found themselves in a large body of water.

"Helmet lights off!" Vision commanded.

The team shut off their lights. Their surroundings went dark again. The water was deep and they could not touch the bottom. Impact and Locust were too heavy to stay afloat for long. They had to flip over onto their backs and use their carapaces like the hull of a boat. The rest of the team had to tread water as Commander Vision looked around with his enhanced eyesight and tried to figure out where they were. The answer was obvious in a few seconds. The giant black bulk of the prison fortress loomed above the Bug Team.

"We're in the lake that surrounds the prison," Vision said as he quickly consulted the rough diagram of the prison on his wrist computer. "It's like a moat."

"How medieval," Impact commented sourly.

"The infiltration point is 30 metres away," Vision said and started to swim slowly towards the sheer walls of the prison. "Mission silence until we're inside."

The lake was more sludge than it was water. The Bug Team's oxygen masks could not even protect them from the vile smell. It was worse than the swamp. There were also unseen . . . things . . . living in the lake that clamped onto Hopper's exposed footpads. He tried to shake them off without making too much of a disturbance in the water. There was no way to know what kind of surveillance was kept on the lake. Even though the team had stealth fields, a simple ripple could betray their presence. Hopper gritted his teeth and kept mission silence as he swam.

He wasn't the only one. All the Bug Team members felt the things latch onto the fabric of their combat uniforms. Apparently their stealth fields were not effective against the creatures. When the Bug Team finally crawled out of the water, they saw that they were covered in leeches of all sizes. But they did not have time to remove them. They had arrived at the infiltration coordinates and had to get inside the prison as fast as possible to keep from being seen.

A single opening in the black, featureless wall of the fortress faced them. It was a large sewer drain that spewed waste from the prison fortress and into the moat. Suddenly, the Bug Team knew what they had been swimming in. It was a septic pool!

Commander Vision led the way up the sluice that channelled the waste from the drain to the lake. The opening had a metal grate welded over it, but Vision had come prepared. The intel had been correct about this

aspect at least. He deployed a cold plasma torch from his combat gear.

Commander Vision began to cut through the bars with the plasma torch. The Bug Team huddled around him and blocked the light emitted by the torch as he worked.

It did not take long for the commander to cut a large hole in the grate. The Bug Team surged through the opening and into the sewer pipe. It was big enough for the team to stand upright. Impact leaned the cut portion of the grate back up against the hole to mask their entry point. Bug Team Alpha followed Commander Vision into the prison fortress.

When he was 30 metres down the pipe Commander Vision punched a special code into his wrist computer. It authorized a single, specific, secure message only to General Barrett. Vision's message contained just two words:

We're in.

On board the Coalition battleship *Ares*, General Barrett received Commander Vision's coded message on his wrist computer.

"They're in," Barrett murmured under his breath and secretly pumped his fist.

The general stood up from his command chair on the bridge. He activated the ship-to-ship comm to address all the vessels in the armada heading towards the Draco home world.

"Attention! We are about to embark on a mission of interstellar importance. Our actions will be recorded and remembered!" General Barrett announced.

"The armada is nearing the coordinates of the Draco solar system, sir. Ready to drop out of hyperspace," the ship's navigator said.

"Sensors indicate Draco ships have massed in a defensive line," the weapons officer informed Barrett.

"Drop out of hyperspace and show the enemy what they're up against," the general ordered. "I want them to see the can of worms they've opened."

CHAPTER 4

The members of Bug Team Alpha picked the leeches off their uniforms as they sloshed further into the sewer system that ran through the bowels of the prison. They turned off their stealth fields and turned on their lights. None of them took off their oxygen masks.

Hopper applied antiseptic gel from his emergency medical pack to the places on his exposed footpads where the leeches had drawn blood.

There was no telling what kind of germs the creatures carried. Not only that, the putrid sewer water was full of waste that could cause an infection.

Commander Vision led the team through the large main tunnel. The plan was to follow the main pipe to where it met the prison's central pre-treatment holding tank. That was where all of the bodily waste and rubbish from the prison was collected before being released into the sewer system and out into the septic moat. The tank had an access hatch they could use to enter the sewage facility inside the prison.

The team would launch their rescue mission from this attack position. But Vision did not have a map of the exact route to the holding tank. The mission intel was not able to provide the commander with that important piece.

"I haven't seen any security sensors so far," Vision mentioned as he used his compound eyes to scan the walls of the tunnel.

"The Draco probably don't think they need them. Who would be crazy enough to be down here?" Scorpion said.

"Besides us, you mean," Locust commented.

"Hey, we're not crazy!" Hopper protested. "Just dedicated."

The Bug Team sloshed through the main sewer pipe. They passed several large side-conduits along the way, which emptied liquid and who-knew-what-else into the main tunnel.

"I'm getting vibes of lots of small animals running through the water," Radar mentioned as her cranial antennae twitched, scanning ahead of the team. "I think they must be rats. Or something similar to rats."

"Ugh. I hate rats," Impact shuddered.

The light from the team's gear reflected back from dozens of small pairs of eyes in the dark. The water rippled and moved as the creatures scattered into the side tunnels at the approach of the Bug Team members.

"See, Impact? They're more afraid of you than you are of them," Burrow assured his teammate.

"No. I think they're more afraid of that!" Radar warned.

Suddenly, the head of a gigantic snake appeared in the beams of their lights. It was almost as large as the sewer tunnel. A wave of sludge water surged ahead of the creature as it slithered through the tunnel towards the seven Bug Team Alpha members. The team

automatically took aim at the huge beast with their blasters.

"Hold your fire! I don't want a firefight down here. We don't know how the sound carries," Vision said. "Fall back. Take cover in one of the side tunnels a few metres back and let it pass."

The Bug Team started to retreat slowly.

"How did you miss the vibes of that thing?" Vision whispered to Radar.

"Sorry, sir. It wasn't moving at first. I thought it was a wall," Radar replied.

The giant reptile licked the air with its tongue, using it to sense for prey. It smelled the sewer-saturated scents of the Bug Team and hesitated. Then it "tasted" their body heat. The creature surged forwards.

"Okay, I guess we're going to find out how sound carries down here. Open fire!" Vision ordered.

The huge snake was an easy target but a tough one. The Bug Team fired their blasters point-blank at the snake's head. Its hard scales protected it from immediate damage.

"Aim for its eyes!" Vision instructed.

The reptile's clear, protective eyelid scales saved its eyes from physical harm, but not from the brightness of the energy blasts. Its large irises shrank to slits.

"It can't see us! Impact, Scorpion! Move in!" Vision ordered.

Impact ran towards the dazzled reptile like a bulldozer. She rammed the creature on its nose. It opened its mouth and hissed instinctively.

That's when Scorpion raced forwards and struck the soft, exposed flesh of the creature's tongue with her buglike spikes. Powerful knockout venom was injected into the snake.

"Say *ahhhhh*," Vision said as he followed behind Scorpion and tossed a grenade right into the creature's mouth and down its throat.

Impact grabbed both the commander and Scorpion and ran back towards the rest of her teammates. They were already running down the tunnel to get out of range.

BLOOOMF!

The explosion was muffled by the snake's own body as the grenade detonated. Radar curled up her antennae to protect them from the concussive waves of the blast. Impact used the carapace on her back to shield her teammates from flying blobs of snake guts. The sewer water gained a new layer of stink.

"Well, that was a first," Burrow mentioned as the team walked back to the creature's corpse.

"The Draco didn't need any security monitors because that thing was already down here," Scorpion said.

"Um, how are we going to get past it? It's blocking the whole tunnel," Locust observed.

Commander Vision pulled out the cold plasma cutting torch.

"We go through it," Vision said. "This is going to get messy."

Bug Team Alpha got an unplanned lesson in giant snake anatomy as they took turns carving their way through the reptilian corpse. The creature turned out to be larger than they thought. Its body stretched down the tunnel for almost 20 metres. By the time the team reached the tail, they were covered in stuff that put the smells of the sewer to shame.

"I think I have snake guts in places I didn't know I had places," Scorpion moaned.

"The Draco won't have to see us coming. They'll smell us coming," Locust commented.

"That's not going to matter in about 40 minutes when the armada shows up," Commander Vision reminded them as he checked a countdown on his wrist computer. "Keep moving."

The Bug Team members finally reached the spot where the main sewer pipe connected to the pre-treatment holding tank. The pipe sloped upwards at a steep angle, which was great for pouring off sludge but lousy for climbing. The outflow was heavy and as swift as a waterfall.

Hopper tried to leap up the cascade by bouncing back and forth against the walls, but the surface was too slimy even for his grasshopperlike legs.

"Burrow, it's up to you to spike your way up there," Vision said.

"Yes, sir," Burrow replied and jabbed his arm spikes into the metal pipe.

The pipe was very thick and Burrow's spikes barely dented it. But they penetrated just far enough to make a series of handholds. Impact used them to brace her feet and support Burrow from behind as he continued upwards. The rest of the team climbed slowly after them.

CHAPTER 5

Bug Team Alpha worked their way up the steep pipe through a waterfall of slimy sludge. Their uniforms were soaked through to their skin. Bits of snake guts hung from their gear. The stink of sewer gases seeped past their oxygen masks and made their stomachs turn. But they were on a mission to rescue the President of Earth from the Draco enemy. Their personal comfort was not important.

There was a grate at the top of the pipe. Commander Vision used the cold plasma torch to cut through it. The team entered the holding tank. It was full of debris flushed from every toilet and sink and drain in the prison. They swam up to the surface.

Vision spotted the service ladder. It was a quick climb up to the access hatch in the roof of the enclosed tank. Vision pulled back the interior latches and slid the hatch sideways on its rusty rails. The hatch made a loud squeal as it moved. Vision froze. He knew that if any Draco heard the noise, the Bug Team would be discovered. This part of the mission was as dangerous as battling the giant sewer snake.

Suddenly, the hatch was wrenched out of Commander Vision's hands and shoved aside by someone on the other side. The commander aimed his blaster at the opening, ready to fire. A face peered down at the Bug Team.

Hopper leaped up from his place on the ladder and straight through the open hatch. He slammed into the unidentified person. He did not know if it was friend or foe.

Vision scrambled up out of the tank and aimed his weapon in a 360 sweep. The Bug Team followed their commander up out of the holding tank and into the sewage processing facility, ready for action. But there was no Draco enemy. There was only a dirt-smeared prisoner lying on the ground with Hopper sitting on his chest.

"You're here at last!" the man wheezed.

"Hold your fire," Vision ordered his team.

Then the commander took a closer look at the man and what he was wearing. He was human with slime-smeared red hair and weary green eyes. His body was thin, but his smile was broad and hopeful. Under the grime was a torn white uniform with a ship's emblem badge that Vision recognized immediately.

"You're from *Space Ship One*!" Vision realized.

"Yes. I'm Julien Stoneman, Chief Steward," the man replied. "We knew the Coalition would send someone to rescue us!"

More prisoners came out from behind the maze of metal plumbing pipes that fed sewage into the holding tank. Among them Vision counted 12 humans in *Space Ship One* uniforms. There were others in the group who were not humans. Most of them were humanoids with features and skin that looked like turtles, frogs and even snails. Commander Vision did not recognize their various species. He concluded that they probably came from planets conquered by the Draco.

"Where are the guards?" Hopper asked as he jumped off Julien's chest and helped him to his feet.

"We took 'em out when they came on shift a few hours ago. The next shift won't arrive for another six Earth Standard hours at least. You've got some time," a slender *Space Ship One* crew woman replied. She was as petite as Lt Radar and held a length of pipe in one hand like a weapon. "No Draco soldier wants guard duty down here. None of them get here on time, and they're lazy when they do."

"Meet Presidential Protective Service agent code-named 'Pompeii.' She's kept us all alive down here," Julien admitted.

"You're assigned to President McCaffrey. Is she down here?" Vision asked.

"No. The rumour is that she's on Level 14," Agent Pompeii replied.

"Rumour?" Vision echoed.

"There is an ongoing information network among prisoners," one of the turtle humanoids said with a thick accent. "Some is true, some is false. Some is free, most is not."

"The higher the information costs, the more reliable it is. Most of the time," Julien shrugged.

"The network pays little for intel, but sells high,"

Pompeii explained. "We wanted to know about President McCaffrey but couldn't even find out whom to contact in the network. But then someone in the network came to us."

"We were offered extra food and water for information about the sewer system and this facility," Julien said. "At first we thought it was about someone in the network gathering info for yet another escape attempt, but they also wanted to know specifically about the *Space Ship One* crew. That's when we dared to hope that someone was coming for us."

"We don't know how the information got to the Coalition, but we're glad it did," Pompeii declared.

"Then our intel about the infiltration point and holding tank probably originated from you and your fellow prisoners," Vision said.

"Well, I wish someone had mentioned the giant sewer snake in that intel," Scorpion said sourly.

"It exists? We thought it was just a story created to stop escape attempts," one of the froglike humanoids gasped.

"Nope. Not a story," Locust replied and picked a string of reptile guts off himself. "But don't worry. We killed it."

"Then we can escape!" one of the turtle prisoners realized.

"Well, yes, you can get out the way we came in, but I wouldn't recommend it," Vision cautioned. "The grates are cut but there are sewer rats and who knows what else in the tunnels. And then there's the septic moat and the perimeter bunkers outside."

"Our freedom is worth the risk," the prisoner declared and started to climb down the service ladder. Other prisoners followed.

Vision checked his wrist computer. He took Agent Pompeii aside and whispered in her ear.

"We're expecting backup in 20. Keep them underground until then. Don't let them out into the marsh," Vision said.

"Understood. Cavalry's coming," Pompeii replied. "You'd better hustle. It's going to take more than 20 minutes to get to Level 14. We're on Sub-Level 10, and there are a lot of Draco guards in between."

"Good to know. Here. You're going to need this," the commander said as he stripped off his oxygen mask and air supply cylinder and gave it to the agent.

The rest of the Bug Team handed over their masks and cylinders to members of the *Space Ship One* crew. Then Agent Pompeii led them down into the holding tank. The hatch closed. Bug Team Alpha was again on its own.

The Coalition battleship *Ares* was the first vessel to drop out of hyperspace at the outer edge of the Draco solar system. They were immediately followed by five battleships, then 10 carriers and 20 destroyers. General Barrett stood on the bridge of the flagship and studied the main monitor screen that displayed the line of opposing Draco warships standing in his way.

The Draco vessels looked like birds of prey with metal wings and tails. The front sections had curved "beaks" that added to the hawklike appearance. Each hull was painted with feathers on the main body and reptilian scales on the front sections.

"Huh. They look like vultures," General Barrett said. "Open a comm channel to the Draco fleet."

"Frequency is open, sir," a communications officer replied.

"Release President McCaffrey, alive and unharmed, along with the crew of *Space Ship One*," Barrett said, short and to the point. "Failure to do so will result in retaliatory action."

The image on the monitor screen shifted and then displayed the face of Histaah, the Supreme Commander of the Dracos Space Fleet.

"The Earth Colonial Coalition will withdraw from the planets newly claimed by the Draco," Histaah insisted. "Failure to do so will result in the immediate death of the captives!"

The monitor screen went black as Histaah severed the comm link.

"Well, it looks like the mission timeline just got moved up," General Barrett said. Then he announced: "All Coalition ships. Engage the enemy. Open fire!"

CHAPTER 6

On the edge of the Draco solar system, the two opposing space fleets bombarded each other with destructive force. Weapons fire from energy cannons streaked through the vacuum like meteorites. Torpedoes exploded like miniature suns.

The Coalition carriers launched individual fighters that zipped under and around enemy fire and peppered the Draco ships. In turn, swarms of Draco strike craft were deployed to combat the Coalition fighters.

The space between the two fleets became a flurry of zooming spacecraft. Debris from destroyed fighters glittered like stars.

"Concentrate fire on the Draco flagship. Take out their leader," General Barrett ordered. "What's that saying? Cut off the head of the snake and the body will die? Very appropriate in this situation."

The battleship *Ares* continued to lead the Coalition armada in relentlessly attacking the enemy flagship. The energy shields of the Draco's ship flickered and almost failed.

Seeing this weakness, Barrett ordered the *Ares* to move in. He sent his ship at full speed towards the Draco vessel.

"Does the human commander think to ram my ship?" Histaah gasped as he watched the *Ares* head straight for him. "He is mad!"

Histaah ordered his crew to return fire with everything in the ship's arsenal. Cannons blazed. Torpedoes erupted. The *Ares* responded in kind, and kept on coming. The exchange formed a sphere of blinding energy between the two ships and expanded until both vessels were swallowed by the great ball of fire.

And then, something inside the flaming sphere blew up.

All the ships in both fleets were shaken by the tremendous shockwave. The small fighter craft were tossed like scraps of paper in a high wind. Even the massive destroyers and carriers felt the impact. The Draco and the Coalition crews paused in shock and surprise. Had both flagships been destroyed?

Then the *Ares* emerged from the fiery holocaust. It was singed and battered, but it was intact. It headed deeper into the Draco solar system, on a direct course for the Draco home world. The Draco flagship was nowhere to be seen.

It only took a few minutes for the *Ares* to reach the planet and settle into orbit. Every Draco ship and fighter followed Barrett's ship and fired on it in a desperate attempt to stop it.

But the Draco lacked organization. Their attacks were wild and uncoordinated. The symbolic snake's head had been severed and the body was flailing.

"It's time to stir things up for Bug Team Alpha. Open fire around the prison coordinates," General Barrett commanded.

Energy blasts from the flagship's cannons streaked towards the planet and struck the swamps surrounding the prison. The guard bunkers were destroyed in the first strike. The barrage was meant as cover fire for Bug Team Alpha, but it also served to clear the way for ground troops to land.

"Launch the first wave of assault troops," General Barrett ordered.

"Dropships are away, sir," an officer said a minute later.

Barrett typed a message onto his wrist computer and transmitted it on a coded, secure channel. It was meant for one person only and contained two words:

"We're coming."

Inside the prison, Bug Team Alpha rode a slow lift up from the sewage facility in the lowest sub-level of the fortress. There were only 10 buttons on the control panel, one for each sub-level. There was no direct route from the sewage facility to Level 14.

Suddenly, the team felt the first salvos from the Coalition armada strike near the prison. The lift shuddered and shook, but it kept moving.

"They're early," Commander Vision muttered.

A message appeared on his wrist computer:

We're coming.

A blast struck close to the fortress. The lift rattled dangerously in its shaft. The lights flickered.

"The general has started the party. Our timetable just got moved up," Vision told the team.

"Well, if his plan was to kick the proverbial hornet's nest and send the Draco swarming, I've got to say that he's doing a great job of kicking," Lt Impact observed.

"It's up to us to use the confusion to find the president and get her to the extraction point ASAP," Burrow added.

They could hear and feel the barrage of cannon fire striking from orbit. Then it increased. Radar curled up her antennae. The lift shook violently. The lights went out as the power failed. The lift stopped between Sub-Levels Five and Six.

"Ride's over. Time to climb," Vision said as he opened the escape hatch in the ceiling of the lift.

The commander was the first one up. He stood on the roof of the lift and looked up the lightless shaft. He used his DNA-enhanced eyes to see that, even though there were only four and a half levels to go, it was still a long way to the top.

"There's a service ladder," the commander said. "Radar, Hopper and Scorpion, start climbing. Helmet lights on!"

Hopper used his bug legs to leap up the rungs five at a time. Scorpion and Radar followed him. Impact, Locust and Burrow struggled to squeeze their bulky bodies through the hatch. Commander Vision waited to use the cold plasma torch to cut them out of the lift if he needed to. But they popped out on their own. Impact and Burrow started to climb the ladder.

"Locust, get me up there, fast," Vision said.

Locust wrapped his arms around his commander and flew him up the lift shaft. When they got to Sub-Level One at the top of the shaft, Vision grabbed onto the ladder next to Radar. There was a closed lift door between the Bug Team and Sub-Level One of the prison. And there was no way to know what was on the other side.

"Radar, can you pick up any vibes about what's beyond that door?" Vision asked.

The lift shaft shook as another heavy salvo from space struck outside the prison fortress. The team gripped the rungs of the ladder to stop them from being thrown off.

"No, sir. The cannon fire is creating too much interference," Radar said. "It's like trying to listen for a whisper in a room full of screaming people."

"Okay, lieutenant. I'm going to pull the door open a little and take a look," Vision decided. "Stand ready, team."

The commander wedged the armoured tips of his combat gloves between the door and its frame. He pulled, but the door barely budged. The commander placed a foot against the doorframe and heaved. The door slid back a few centimetres and Vision put one compound eye up to the small opening.

A blinding flash of blaster fire hit the lift door. Suddenly, Commander Vision saw nothing but pure white light. Then everything went black. The impact from the blast threw the commander back. He lost his hold on the doorframe and began to fall. There was nothing between him and the bottom of the shaft. Except for Locust.

"I've got him!" Locust declared as he buzzed down the shaft and snagged his commander by the sleeve.

Unfortunately, the sewer slime on Locust's gloves didn't let him get a firm grip on the layers of sewage and snake guts on Vision's uniform. The commander slid out of Locust's hand.

CHAPTER 7

"I've got him!" Hopper declared as he hooked a lifeline to the ladder and launched himself down the shaft with his powerful grasshopper legs. It gave him the extra speed to catch up to the commander.

Hopper grabbed Vision and wrapped his arms and extra-long legs around him.

THWAAG!!!

Hopper's rope stopped their fall. The whiplash knocked the breath out of both teammates. When they looked down they saw that the roof of the lift was only a metre below them.

"Could . . . have . . . gone splat," Vision wheezed. He whacked Hopper's shoulder in thanks.

Impact and Burrow combined their strength to quickly pull Vision and Hopper back up the lift shaft on the rope.

Meanwhile, Radar, Locust and Scorpion observed what was happening on the other side of the partially open lift door.

"There's a full-scale prison riot going on out there," Locust said. "Mission 'confusion' accomplished."

More blaster fire exploded near the lift door. Vision grimaced. His eyes were still sensitive from the blast that had almost blinded his DNA-enhanced bug eyes a few minutes before.

"While the Draco guards are busy dealing with the riot, we'll get to the president on Level 14," the commander declared. "Move out."

The Bug Team Alpha members pulled the lift door wide open. They surged out into the chaos of the Draco guards battling against several hundred prisoners.

Sub-Level One was an open room as large as a spacecraft hangar, which allowed Locust to fly aloft and provide recon info.

"I don't see any more lifts, but there's a large armoured door straight ahead," Locust told Vision over the comm. "It's the only way out."

"Head for the doors," the commander ordered.

Impact bulldozed ahead of the team and cleared a path. Hopper used his powerful legs to thump the Draco guards as he encountered them, while Scorpion followed and spiked them with her knockout venom. They would not be getting back up for a while. Vision, Burrow and Radar used their blasters to drop any Draco guards left in their way.

The furious shouts of rioting sputtered and slowed as the prisoners noticed the Bug Team taking out the Draco. Then the shouts became cheers as the prisoners realized that they had help.

Suddenly, a new series of salvos shook the prison fortress from floor to roof. The lights dimmed as the power was disrupted.

"That's Coalition cannon fire. There's an armada in space that's fighting the Draco," Vision shouted to the crowd.

"We can escape!" someone yelled.

A huge hurrah went up. The mob moved towards the large doors Locust had seen earlier. They swarmed the heavy metal doors and started pulling at the hinges and locked latches with their bare hands.

It did not take long for the prisoners to wrench the door off its frame. They poured through the opening and up a set of stairs towards the next level – Main Level One.

In less than a minute, the mob clogged the opening. Bug Team Alpha was left standing on the wrong side of the clog.

"We're not getting through to the upper levels that way," Vision muttered.

As Coalition cannon fire from above continued to shake the fortress, Vision decided that one more explosion would hardly be noticed.

"Locust, blow a hole in the ceiling. We'll get out of here that way," Vision ordered.

Locust buzzed up to the ceiling and attached a couple of grenades. He quickly came back down by his teammates.

BLAAAM!

A few seconds later the Bug Team had a new exit. Locust flew back up and through the hole.

"More rioting up here, sir," Locust reported over the comm.

"Hopper, get up there and help Locust secure drop lines," Vision ordered.

Hopper leaped up through the opening in a single bounce. Ropes dropped down a moment later. As the rest of Bug Team Alpha crawled up the ropes and through the hole, Locust and Hopper provided covering fire to protect the team.

To add to the confusion, the prisoners from Sub-Level One were starting to swarm up onto Main Level One from the stairway. The only exit from the prison was on Main Level One and every prisoner was trying to get there.

The Draco guards fought against the combined riots and barely noticed the Bug Team run, fly and hop through the mayhem towards a bank of lifts.

"There are Draco guards by the lifts," Locust warned over the comm.

"Take them out," Vision ordered.

The Draco guards instinctively froze in surprise at the sight of the half-bug, half-human soldiers charging towards them.

Impact and Locust slammed two of the guards against the lift doors. Hopper kicked another guard into the wall. Scorpion swept in and spiked them with her knockout venom.

There were signs above the lifts that indicated that they went to Levels 1 to 14. The power was out, so Impact used her strength to pry open one of the doors. There was no lift. Vision leaned into the shaft and looked up. The compartment was stuck several levels above Main Level One.

"Looks like we've got another long climb," the commander observed.

CHAPTER 8

The lift shaft was too narrow for Locust to deploy his wings, so he climbed along with the rest of the Bug Team.

Hopper leaped up the rungs of the service ladder ahead of the team. At each level he put his ear to the doors and tried to hear what was happening on the other side.

"I'm no Radar, but it sounds like there's a riot on every level," Hopper reported over the comm.

The Coalition cannon fire continued outside the prison as the Bug Team climbed. The service ladder vibrated under their grip. Suddenly, the team was rocked by a blast that had nothing to do with the Coalition bombardment. The lift door one level below them blew open.

Blaster fire exploded into the shaft and bounced off the walls. It was followed by a gush of prisoners pouring through the breach. Some of them grabbed the service ladder and half-fell, half-climbed down the rungs. Others leaped into the shaft and grabbed the lift's vertical rails and slid down them to the levels below. No one looked up. Their goal was to reach the exit on Main Level One. None of the prisoners noticed the Bug Team steadily climbing above them.

The team finally reached the stalled lift compartment at Level 10. There was a slim space between the compartment and the service ladder. Radar, Hopper and Scorpion were the right size to squeeze through, but Impact, Burrow and Locust were too big.

"Scorpion, Radar, Hopper. Keep climbing. I'll cut through the bottom of the lift so that the rest of us can go up through the compartment. We'll climb out of the ceiling hatch," Vision said as he pulled out the cold plasma torch.

Hopper, Radar and Scorpion started climbing as Vision started cutting.

As Hopper reached the top of the lift compartment, he saw a Draco guard helping another one up out of the escape hatch.

"We've got Draco in the lift," Hopper warned over the comm as he fired his blaster at the enemy.

Hopper's shot hit one of the Draco guards, who dropped back down into the compartment, unconscious. The second guard returned fire, but Hopper leaped off the ladder, sailed over the Draco's head, and grabbed onto the vertical lift rails on the wall of the shaft. As the guard turned to follow Hopper with his weapon, Scorpion came up from behind and spiked him.

Hopper dropped back down onto the roof as Radar and Scorpion aimed their weapons down into the hatch. More reptilian Draco faces looked up at them. The enemy fired on the Bug Team.

Meanwhile, Vision finished cutting the hole in the bottom floor of the lift compartment. The plate fell away and suddenly the Draco looked down and faced the large, bug eyes of Commander Vision, just before they fell to his blaster fire.

"Hopper, Radar, Scorpion, keep climbing. We're right behind you," Vision said as he, Impact, Burrow and Locust climbed up through the hole in the floor of the lift compartment.

Hopper bounced up the ladder as his teammates followed. Impact, Burrow and Locust wriggled their large bodies out of the escape hatch and climbed up after them. Vision paused inside the lift long enough to gather the Draco guards' weapons and clip them to his combat belt. Then the commander snagged one of their comm units and fitted it over his ear. Now he could listen to the Draco comm chatter. What he heard alarmed him:

"Execute the prisoners!"

"Move the Earth president!"

"Kill the Earth president!"

"Destroy Level 14!"

Commander Vision could not tell which message was coming from which Draco authority. It sounded as if the whole command structure was disorganized and confused.

"They're acting like a snake with its head cut off," Vision muttered.

In his other ear, Vision could hear the comm chatter from the Coalition forces. He listened to General Barrett and the battalion commanders on the dropships landing near the prison fortress. The Coalition cannon fire had lessened in the last few minutes. Now Vision knew why. It was to make way for ground troops.

"The cavalry has arrived," the commander realized as he hauled himself out of the lift escape hatch and started to climb up the service ladder after his team to Level 14. Vision hoped that the President of Earth was still there when Bug Team Alpha arrived.

The first Coalition dropships started to land in the marshes and swamps surrounding the Draco prison. Hundreds of Draco warriors had arrived in response to the Coalition bombardment and the threat of invading troops.

The majority of the soldiers came from a military base close to the prison. The rest of the fighters were private militia from nearby towns, and some even came out of retirement to defend their world.

The Draco had a proud and glorious history of warfare, and none of them could pass up a good fight. They raced to the swamps surrounding the prison to engage the enemy.

The heavy Coalition vessels sank into the unstable soil, just like the Bug Team's stealth ship – only worse. The dropships sank so low into the muck that they could not open their troop deployment ramps.

The Draco took full advantage of their enemy's difficulty. This was their home world, and they were perfectly suited to combat in these conditions. Their methods of swamp warfare were developed over centuries.

In their barbarian days, the Draco had tamed giant reptilian creatures that resembled dragons to ride into battle. Now they used mechanical replicas of those beasts. A wave of Draco warriors on aerodynamic, anti-grav "dragons" charged the floundering Coalition dropships. The militia and retirees used footgear that looked like mini pontoons to run on the surface of the water.

The mounted Draco warriors swarmed around the Coalition dropships and fired energy blasts at the vessels that were stuck in the mud. Their weapons looked more like ancient spears than modern blasters. They threw grenades that exploded upon contact with the hulls of the dropships.

BOOOOM!

BWAAAM!

Thick clouds of smoke erupted. One of the dropships abruptly tipped to one side. The Draco warriors cheered in victory. But the Coalition hulls were tougher than the Draco realized. The Draco assault did not make a dent.

Suddenly, the Coalition dropships fired their engines and lifted up out of the marsh. Blasts of swamp water and muck flew in the faces of the Draco.

The warriors and their mechanical dragons fell backwards. The militia and retirees were knocked off their floating feet. Even though they were tossed and thrown down into the marsh, the Draco cheered. The Coalition ships were fleeing! The enemy was retreating!

But the dropships did not leave. They stopped and hovered above the soggy marsh. Although landing on solid ground was preferable, and conserved fuel, the vessels didn't really need it. The deployment ramps lowered, and Coalition troops charged out of the dropships on anti-grav megacycles known as Hover Hogs with blasters blazing.

The Draco warriors struggled in the mud where they had fallen during the engine blasts. The Coalition troops overwhelmed their enemy strategically and in superior numbers. Even though the Draco were proud and skilled warriors, they knew when they were defeated. They honourably gave up their weapons in surrender.

Then the Coalition forces headed towards the prison fortress.

CHAPTER 9

Bug Team Alpha climbed up the last few levels of the prison lift shaft and finally reached Level 14 of the maximum-security fortress.

To get there, they had slogged through the swamps of Dracos, sloshed through putrid sewer pipes and confronted a giant tunnel snake. They had swum in raw sewage and run the gauntlet of a massive prison riot.

Now only a single closed lift door stood between the Bug Team and the completion of their mission to rescue the President of Earth.

Impact attempted to pry open the door with her DNA-enhanced strength. She was the strongest member of Bug Team Alpha, but the door did not budge. Burrow and Locust tried to help, but the door did not open.

"It might have been sealed shut from the inside. This is not good," Commander Vision realized as he deployed the cold plasma torch.

As Vision used the torch to cut through the lift door, the rest of the team aimed their blasters and were ready for whatever was on the other side.

The cut panel fell into a large room. There was no answering weapon fire. Impact barrelled through the hole. Locust followed. They both turned in a 360-degree sweep, looking for the Draco enemy or other opposition.

They didn't see either. All they saw were rows of cells filled with agitated prisoners. Commander Vision and the rest of the team stepped through the lift doors and onto Level 14.

"Where are the guards?" Burrow asked.

"It looks like they ran away," Scorpion said.

"Find the president," Vision ordered and started to jog down a row of prison cells.

Non-human prisoners occupied all of the cells. Just like down in the sewage facility, these were captives from other planetary systems the Draco had conquered. They pounded on the metal grates that held them inside the cells and shouted to be let out. Scorpion set a small grenade on the lock of one of the cells and blew open the door.

"Thank you!" the prisoner exclaimed as he rushed out of the cell. "Who are you? What's happening?"

"We're Bug Team Alpha, and you're being rescued," Scorpion replied. She slapped a few grenades into the hands of the prisoner. "Use these to blow the locks open and free the others."

Commander Vision skidded to a stop in front of a cell that had a human prisoner inside. The woman's clothes were ripped and dirty, but they were from Earth. Vision used his blaster to shoot the electronic lock off the cell door.

"Are you from *Space Ship One*?" Vision asked.

"Yes! Yes! I'm Dyanna LeGuin, Special Adviser to the President of Earth! I'm so glad you're here!" the woman replied breathlessly.

"Where's President McCaffrey?" Vision wanted to know.

"I . . . I don't know. She wasn't on my row," LeGuin replied.

Vision unhooked the Draco blasters from his belt and shoved them into the adviser's arms.

"Free as many prisoners as you can," Vision said and raced on.

Then the commander told his team over the comm: "There's a *Space Ship One* survivor in here – one of the president's advisers. There might be more. Find them. Find the president!"

"Yes, sir!" came the reply from all.

Level 14 turned out to be as large as the others, but this one was different. It was divided into many sections, each with rows of individual cells. It took a long time to search them all. Too long as far as Commander Vision was concerned.

"Commander! I found a guy who knows where the president is!" Burrow's voice came over the team's comm. "He's not from *Space Ship One*, but –"

"Where?" Vision demanded.

"The roof, Commander. The Draco guards took her to the roof," Burrow replied. "The stairs are in the southeast quadrant of this level."

"Bug Team Alpha! Converge on the southeast quadrant!" Vision ordered.

The Bug Team arrived at the door to the stairwell. There was an electronic lock on the door. That did not stop them.

Vision blew the lock with a grenade. Impact wrenched the door open, almost pulling it off its hinges. Hopper immediately bounced up the stairwell, followed by Commander Vision. The rest of the team was right behind them.

Suddenly, they heard an exchange of blaster fire. When the rest of the team joined Hopper, they saw that he was pinned down behind the half-open door to the roof.

"I saw President McCaffrey. There are about 10 Draco guards and one civilian surrounding her," Lt Hopper said. "It looks like they are going to attempt to load her onto a helicopter that's on its way in for landing."

"We make this surgical," Vision declared. "Scorpion, Burrow, shoot left. Radar and I will shoot right. Impact, Hopper, down the middle. Locust, go aloft and grab the president."

Vision shoved the door open.

"Go! Go! Go!"

Bug Team Alpha surged out of the doorway and split in four directions. The Draco guards didn't know where to shoot first.

Those few seconds of confusion gave the Bug Team the tactical advantage. Impact charged straight towards the Draco guards holding President McCaffrey. Hopper bounded across the roof in a few quick leaps. Vision blasted two guards on the right. Radar dropped another. Scorpion wasn't close enough to the enemy to use her knockout venom. Her blaster was just as effective.

The Draco response was to shoot wildly and at random. They were prison guards, not trained soldiers. They did not have a commander. The only Draco in their midst who might be considered a leader was the prison warden, and he was lying on his face with his hands over his head.

The Draco helicopter paused in its approach to the prison roof. The vehicle looked like a dragon with helicopter rotors. It was painted and plated with reptilian scales. Locust banked past the cockpit window and waved at the pilot just before he swooped down towards the president.

Suddenly, a blast from a Draco weapon hit Locust. He fell out of the air and rolled across the roof of the prison. He did not get up.

"Noooo!" Hopper yelled as he saw his teammate fall. He leaped towards the Draco guard who had shot his friend and kicked him with the full force of his grasshopper DNA-enhanced legs. The guard was tossed across the length of the prison roof, through the doorway, and down the stairwell.

Hopper turned back towards President McCaffrey and saw that the warden now threatened her with a blaster. The remaining prison guards surrounded the warden and the president in a protective circle as the helicopter came back towards the roof for a landing.

Commander Vision knew if President McCaffrey got onto that Draco transport his mission would be a failure.

"It's mission critical! Heads up!" Vision shouted a warning to his team as he snagged a grenade from his belt and threw it towards the President of Earth.

The warden and the guards could not believe what they were seeing. They instinctively let go of McCaffrey and leaped away from the grenade.

But the president was not Vision's target. The grenade zipped past McCaffrey's head and into the open boarding hatch of the descending helicopter.

Hopper leaped forwards in one powerful bounce and grabbed the president. A second bounce carried them away from the Draco and the helicopter.

At the same time, Impact charged the aircraft as it hovered above the roof. She slammed into the side of its hull and knocked it sideways. Its rotor blades could not catch air. The vehicle tipped over and started to drop down the side of the prison fortress. Then Vision's grenade exploded.

CHAPTER 10

The Draco vessel erupted into flames as it fell down the side of the prison. It landed in the septic moat surrounding the fortress and blew up some more. Then the sludge caught on fire.

The warden and the remaining guards realized there was no escape for them now. Their transport was destroyed and the only way off the roof was to go through the strange-looking humans. And even if they got past the humans, there was a whole prison full of rioting captives between them and the exit on Main Level One. The warden dropped his weapon and raised his hands in the universal sign of surrender. But the guards were not ready to give up. The five remaining Draco prison guards threw down their blasters and pulled bladed short swords from their belts. Then they rushed at the Bug Team.

"Those guys are crazy," Hopper observed as he stood on the far side of the roof protecting President McCaffrey.

Bug Team Alpha met the challenge. They engaged the Draco in hand-to-hand combat. The Draco slashed at them with razor-sharp battle blades. The swords were an ancient and traditional part of the guards' uniforms, but they were still deadly weapons.

Commander Vision blocked a sword blow with his blaster, and then used it to shove the Draco blade aside. Then he kicked the feet out from under his opponent. As the Draco fell, Vision smacked him on the head with the butt of his blaster in one smooth motion. The Draco did not get up.

Scorpion spun out of the path of the guard running towards her and spiked him in the neck as he passed. He took a few steps before he fell.

Impact simply used her immense strength to punch the guard who was charging her. The Draco guard dropped his sword and then dropped to the ground.

Burrow blocked his enemy's sword blow with the tough spikes of his right arm, and then punched the guard with his left. The Draco had a sturdy chin and came back for more. As they faced off, Impact picked up the guard she had knocked out and threw him at the Draco confronting Burrow. The guard was suddenly bowled over by the unconscious body. The two tangled and rolled across the roof. They did not get up.

Meanwhile, Radar zigzagged out of the reach of her opponent's sword swipes. She avoided contact by using her antennae to feel the vibrations of his muscles as they moved, as well as the displacement the blade made in the air.

The Draco got very frustrated and lost his concentration. That's when Radar moved in as swift as a cobra. She grabbed his weapon wrist and twisted it sharply. The sword fell from the Draco's numb fingers. She continued to twist and the guard's whole body followed. He suddenly found himself on the ground looking up at his opponent. It was the last thing he saw before Radar delivered a karate blow to the nerves in his neck.

The Bug Team shackled the unconscious guards with the Draco's own prison restraints. The warden was tied up with a cord from Vision's combat belt. Once the roof was secure, the rest of the Bug Team surrounded President McCaffrey. Hopper was finally able to run over to the fallen form of Locust. He expected the worst. But Locust opened his eyes and sat up, only dazed.

"What did I miss?" Locust asked.

Hopper helped his friend to his feet. Locust looked around at the captured Draco and then over the side of the roof at the flaming remains of the helicopter.

"Not much," Hopper shrugged.

"Are you fit to fly?" Vision asked Locust.

"Yes, sir!" Locust assured the commander.

"Good. Get President McCaffrey back to the stealth ship and up to the armada," Vision said as he strapped his stealth gear onto the president and activated it. The president became a blur. "The rest of the Bug Team will catch another ride."

"Yes, sir!" Lt Locust said as he wrapped his arms around McCaffrey. Then he activated his own stealth gear and took off. The pair was invisible in the night, and the sound of his wings was drowned out by the sounds of battle all around the prison below them.

Commander Vision typed in a secure, coded message on his wrist computer to General Barrett. It contained three words: "We have her."

"Okay, team, our job's not done yet," Vision declared and hauled the bound prison warden to his feet. "Grab the guards and take 'em downstairs. They're going to help us locate the rest of the *Space Ship One* crew."

The rest of Bug Team Alpha returned to Level 14. They expected to find it in the middle of a riot just like all the other levels of the prison, but it was calm and organized. The inmates here were making plans to take command of the lower levels and organize the other prisoners.

"Well, this is different!" Burrow blurted.

"Level 14 is where the Draco keep all the captured military officers and other high-ranking, high-value prisoners," Dyanna LeGuin explained. "They're the commanding officers and leaders of most of the beings imprisoned on the lower levels."

"We're helping to liberate the oppressed species the Draco have imprisoned here," adviser Ramona Fraydon exclaimed enthusiastically.

"We're making new friends and allies!" LeGuin agreed.

"Hey, everybody! The warden is here with some

of his pals! Let's show them the same hospitality they showed us!" adviser Fraydon shouted.

A crowd surrounded Bug Team Alpha and relieved them of their Draco captives.

The Coalition battleship *Ares* orbited the planet Dracos without opposition. The Draco space fleet was in tatters. On the ground, the Draco warriors had either surrendered or retreated. The prison inmates had formed small armies on each level and taken control of the fortress. All of *Space Ship One*'s survivors had been found and recovered. It was discovered that the two missing crew members were saboteurs who had caused the explosion on the presidential ship. They had died in the explosion.

Locust had successfully flown President McCaffrey back to the stealth ship and safely delivered her to General Barrett's flagship. A short time later, the rest of Bug Team Alpha arrived on the *Ares* aboard one of the returning troop ships. As promised, Commander Vision had found another ride. Now Bug Team Alpha stood before President McCaffrey and General Barrett in his office aboard the *Ares*.

"My Protective Service agents Pompeii and Vesuvius have led two separate groups of *Space Ship One* survivors to safety aboard the *Ares*," McCaffrey said. "And now my advisers Fraydon and LeGuin are coordinating efforts to relocate the prisoners . . . no, refugees . . . to Earth Colonial Coalition planets until they can return safely to their home worlds."

"The Dracos Space Fleet doesn't have a leader anymore. Their surviving ships have scattered," General Barrett said. "Without a fleet, the Draco expansion into Coalition territory has stopped. And I plan to keep it that way."

"What started out as a disaster has turned into a success. The disaster was the unprovoked attack by the Draco on the Earth Colonial Coalition and its president. That has been defeated," McCaffrey declared.

"Squashed like a bug," Burrow snorted under his breath.

"But the success is the fact that doors have been opened to new diplomatic relations between the Coalition and the worlds hoping to break free from the

Draco," the president said. "And that's thanks to you, Bug Team Alpha. You saved me, the survivors of *Space Ship One*, and countless prisoners held captive by the Draco."

The President of Earth attached awards to their fresh, clean uniforms. She shook their hands – extra carefully with Scorpion – and then leaned in and whispered: "And thanks for taking a shower."

TOP SECRET AND CONFIDENTIAL

TO: GENERAL JAMES CLAUDIUS BARRETT, COMMANDER OF COLONIAL ARMED FORCES

FROM: COMMANDER JACKSON BOONE, BUG TEAM ALPHA

SUBJECT: AFTER ACTION REPORT

MISSION DETAILS:
  Mission Planet: Dracos
  Mission Parameters: Infiltration and rescue
  Mission Team: Bug Team Alpha [BTA]
  * Commander Jackson "Vision" Boone
  * Lt Irene "Impact" Mallory
  * Lt Akiko "Radar" Murasaki
  * Lt Liu "Hopper" Yu
  * Lt Gustav "Burrow" Von Braun
  * Lt Madhuri "Scorpion" Singh
  * Lt Sancho "Locust" Castillo

MISSION SUMMARY:
High Covert Mission

President Lessa McCaffrey and crew of *Space Ship One* captured by enemy forces of Draco Empire. Personnel taken to planet Dracos and held in high security prison. BTA deployed to infiltrate prison and extricate President McCaffrey.

Intel on conditions of prison surroundings was incomplete. BTA encountered unreported heavy marsh, swamp and septic moat. Prison infiltration point achieved and entered. BTA encountered giant sewer snake in tunnels under the prison. This suggests that other such "natural" defences exist in other Draco facilities.

BTA navigated through sewers and reached attack position in prison sewage facility. Survivors of *Space Ship One* encountered in sewage facility. *SSO* captives informed BTA that President McCaffrey was being held on the top level of the Draco prison. *SSO* personnel and other Draco captives then initiated escape back through sewer tunnels cleared by BTA.

Upon initiation of orbital cover fire from Colonial Armed Forces armada, BTA reached upper levels of Draco prison. Upon arrival, BTA was informed that President McCaffrey was being evacuated from the facility by its warden. BTA intercepted and engaged Draco prison guards, warden and Draco transport vessel. Recovery of President McCaffrey achieved. President safely returned to CAF flagship by Lt Sancho "Locust" Castillo.

APPENDIX 1: EQUIPMENT REQUISITION
Stealth Ship (unnamed, unregistered): 1
Personal Stealth Fields: 7
Cold Plasma Torch: 1

APPENDIX 2: PARTICIPANTS:
Bug Team Alpha (mission participants listed above)
25 *Space Ship One* passengers and crew, including:
President of Earth, Lessa McCaffrey
Agent Pompeii, presidential protective service agent
Agent Vesuvius, presidential protective service agent
Presidential advisers Dyanna LeGuin; Ramona Fraydon

END REPORT

Glossary

armada a large group of warships

coordinate measurement used to identify an exact position

DNA molecule that carries all of the instructions to make a living thing and keep it working; DNA is short for deoxyribonucleic acid

grenade small explosive device that is often thrown at enemy targets

hull main body or casing of a hovercraft, boat, ship, tank or tanklike armoured vehicle

infiltration secretly passing into enemy territory to gain information or access

proverbial well-known

salvo releasing several bombs or rocket fire at one time

stealth ability to move without being detected

warden person in charge of a prison

Laurie S Sutton has been interested in science fiction ever since she first saw the *Sputnik* satellite speed across the night sky as a very young child. By 12 years old, she was reading books by classic sci-fi authors Robert Heinlein, Isaac Azimov and Arthur C Clarke. Then she discovered *STAR TREK*.

Laurie's love of outer space has led her to write *STAR TREK* comics for *DC* Comics, *Malibu* Comics and *Marvel* Comics. From her home in Florida, USA, she has watched many Space Shuttle launches blaze a trail though the sky. Now she watches the night sky as the International Space Station sails overhead instead of *Sputnik*.

About the illustrator

James Nathaniel is a digital comic book artist and illustrator from the UK. With a graphics tablet and pen, he produces dramatic narrative focused fantasy, science fiction and non-fiction work. His work is the result of inspiration accumulated from the likes of Sean Gordon Murphy, Jake Wyatt, Jamie Hewlett and Jon Foster, as well as many years playing video games and watching films. In the near future, James hopes to write and illustrate his own graphic novels from stories he's been developing over the years.

Discussion questions

1. The Draco are a people rooted in a long-standing warrior tradition. Do you think this justifies their actions? Explain why or why not.

2. When did the Draco's specialized combat gear and fighter ships help them? When did they not help? What are the strengths and weaknesses of Bug Team Alpha's fighting abilities? Explain your answer.

3. How well do you think the Draco were running the prison? What do you think life was like for the prisoners? Use examples from the text in your answer.

Writing prompts

1. Imagine you were a member of Bug Team Alpha. What bug or insect would you model your new body after? Using descriptive language, write about what physical features and elite fighting skills you would have.

2. Throughout the story, Bug Team Alpha doesn't always know what challenges will lie ahead. At every turn, they had to be prepared for anything. Write about a time you were in a situation in which you weren't sure what the outcome was going to be. How did you prepare yourself for the unknown? How did you feel?

3. What happens next in the story? You decide! Write the next chapter in the story explaining what happens next to Bug Team Alpha, the President of Earth, the recently freed prisoners or the Draco people.

BUG TEAM ALPHA

When an archaeologist goes missing and presumed kidnapped during an expedition, Bug Team Alpha is called in to help.

The president of Earth has been kidnapped by Draco warrior forces. Can Bug Team Alpha rescue her in time?

Talos is under attack, but no one can see exactly who - or what - the enemy is. Bug Team Alpha is called in to fight.

What happens when Bug Team Alpha's transport ship crash lands after intersecting an interplanetary war zone? Read *Stranded* to find out!